WALTER

WALTER

by Laura Joffe Numeroff

MACMILLAN PUBLISHING CO., INC.
New York

COLLIER MACMILLAN PUBLISHERS
London

For a very special person,
my sister Emily

Copyright © 1978 Laura Joffe Numeroff

Macmillan Publishing Co., Inc.
866 Third Avenue, New York, N.Y. 10022
Collier Macmillan Canada, Ltd.

Printed in the United States of America

10   9   8   7   6   5   4   3   2   1

LIBRARY OF CONGRESS CATALOGING IN PUBLICATION DATA
Numeroff, Laura Joffe.
    Walter.
    SUMMARY: The adventures of an absent-minded small
boy who never looks where he is going.
    I. Title.
PZ7.N964Wal   [E]   77-10343
ISBN 0-02-768190-4

This is Walter in his favorite hat.

Walter was always daydreaming.
"Walter, you must be careful,"
his mother told him over and over.
"Watch where you are going
and stop daydreaming all the time,"
his father said.
"O.K.," said Walter.

One day Walter was walking home
from his friend Ralph's house,
with a balloon Ralph had given him.
As usual, he was daydreaming.

He fell into a hole that was being dug for a well
in Mrs. Bixby's backyard.
He tried to climb out, but couldn't.

He tried jumping, but he still couldn't get out.

So he sat for a while. Then he heard a voice.

"Hey, you wanna play house?"

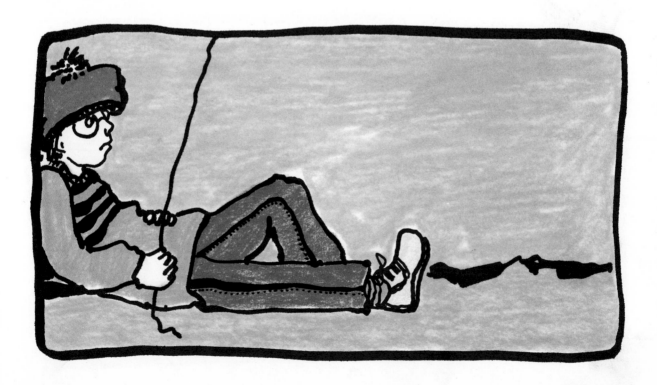

He looked up and saw a little girl
staring down at him.
"No, I don't want to play house," he said.
"I want to get out of this hole."
"Aw, you're no fun," she said.
And she walked away.

Walter said to himself,

"If I ever get out of this hole,

I will <u>never</u> daydream again."

"Hey, Walter, do you always stand in a hole

when you fly a balloon?"

This time it was Bernie, a boy in Walter's class.

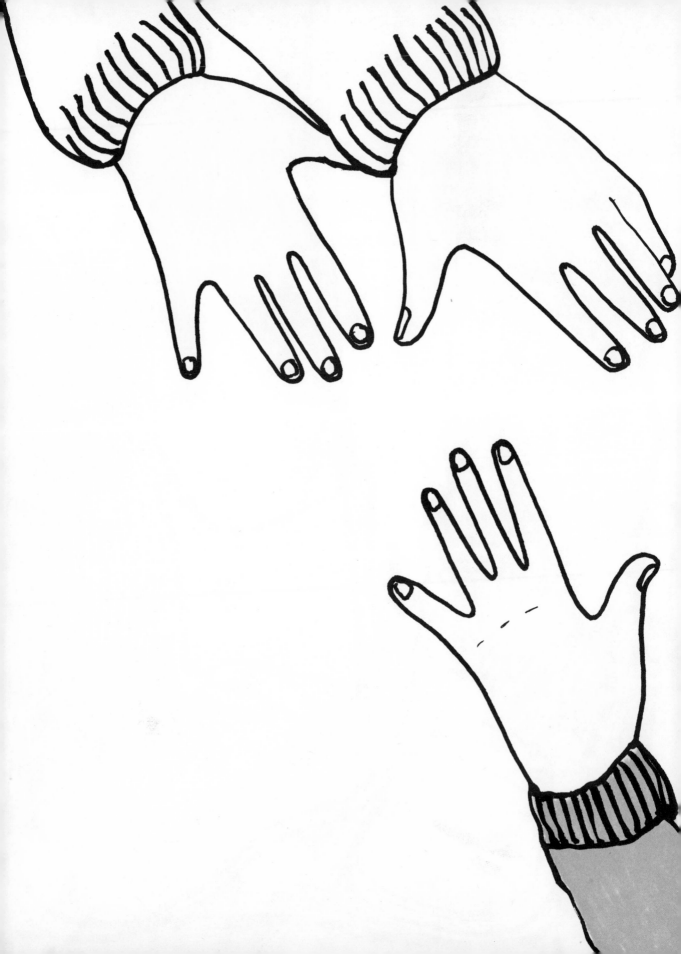

"Get me out of here, Bernie," Walter shouted.
Bernie leaned down,
but his arms weren't long enough.
"Get someone bigger," Walter yelled.

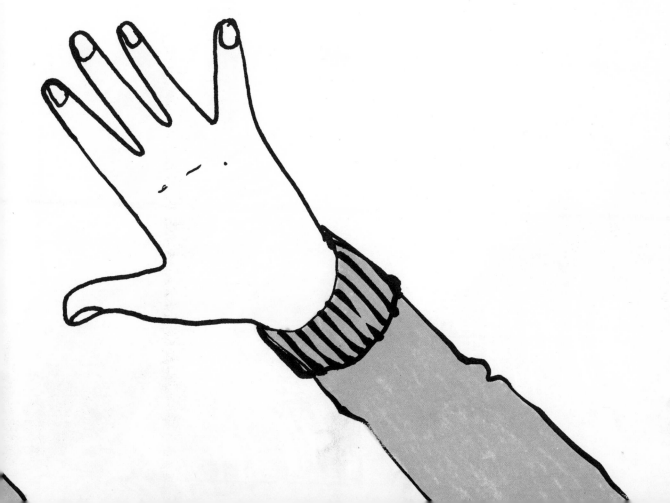

Bernie left and came back with his cousin Lester.
But Lester was only an inch taller than Bernie.
He couldn't reach Walter either.

Several kids had gathered around the hole.

They all tried to get Walter out,

but none of them could reach him.

Walter began to cry.

"I'll never get out of here. I'll miss dinner."

Then Lester said, "I'll hold on to Bernie,
and Bernie can hold on to Ethel,
and Ethel can hold on to Julie,
and Julie can hold on to Arthur,

and Arthur can hold on to Larry,
and then maybe we can reach Walter."

They tried Lester's idea. It didn't work.

Then they tried holding on
to one end of a branch
and having Walter
grab the other.
That didn't work either.

By then, all the noise had awakened
Mrs. Bixby, who had been taking a nap.

She looked out of her window.
"What's going on out there?"
Ethel said, "Walter Weisberg
is stuck in the hole, Mrs. Bixby."
"Oh, dear," she said.
"I'll call his parents."

Walter's parents came
and pulled him out of the hole.

All the kids said good-by
and went home to dinner.

"Walter must have been daydreaming again,"
his mother said to his father.

"He's going to have to be more careful,"
said Walter's father.

But Walter wasn't there.

jE

Numeroff
Walter.

51956

jE

Numeroff
Walter.

51956
(6.95)

1986